THE
HAT
FULL
OF
SECRETS

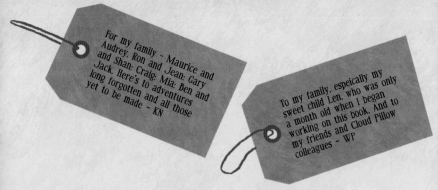

For my family – Maurice and
Audrey, Ron and Jean; Gary
and Shan; Craig; Mia; Ben and
Jack. Here's to adventures
long forgotten and all those
yet to be made ~ KN

To my family, especially my
sweet child Len, who was only
a month old when I began
working on this book. And to
my friends and Cloud Pillow
colleagues ~ WP

STRIPES PUBLISHING LIMITED
An imprint of the Little Tiger Group
1 Coda Studios, 189 Munster Road, London SW6 6AW

Imported into the EEA by Penguin Random House Ireland,
Morrison Chambers, 32 Nassau Street, Dublin D02 YH68

First published in Great Britain in 2020 by Stripes Publishing Limited
This edition published in 2022

This Little Tiger book belongs to:

_____

_____

KARL NEWSON & WAZZA PINK

THE HAT FULL OF SECRETS

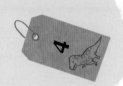

LiTTLE TiGER
LONDON

CHAPTER 1

Henry Pepper didn't ask for it.

He didn't wish it.

He didn't even dream it up.

But there it was...

A secret.

It was the kind of secret that is hard to ignore. The kind that finds you when you're not looking for it. The kind that catches you in the middle of thinking about dinosaurs and unicorns

and your favourite

treble-scoop chocolate

ice cream dessert.

At first, Henry didn't believe his eyes.
He gave them a rub and then looked
again to check if the secret was real.

YES. It was.

And it was a big one at that. Slowly
and quietly, Henry crept back
out of the bushes. Then he
turned and ran as fast
as he could...

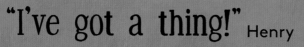
"I've got a thing!" Henry burst through the back door of number 25 and said everything at once and in the wrong order. "There's it. The thing! Is it there?"

"What's all this about a thing?" asked an old man sitting at the kitchen table.

Henry tried again.

"Grandad... There's a thing. I've got. It's!"

Somehow Grandad understood exactly what Henry was trying to say.

"Ah, one of those, is it?" He patted the chair beside him for Henry to sit down. "I had a thing once. Kept me on my toes for weeks! But you know what your mum would say, don't you?" continued Grandad. "There'll be no secrets in this family!" He wagged his finger.

"I just don't know what to do with it ...
that's all," said Henry.

"You can tell me,
if you like?" offered Grandad.

"But,"
Henry replied,

"it
might
eat
you
up!"

"A big one, eh?" said Grandad. "Well, if it's going to worry you that much I'd rather you did tell me, but only when you're ready. Or..." he paused for a moment, "...you could keep it under your hat – so long as you've done no wrong, it'll do no harm there."

"My hat?"

said Henry, itching a thought out of his head.

There was just one problem.
"I don't have a hat."

"YOU
DON'T
HAVE A
HAT?!"

Grandad spluttered
on his cup of tea
and spat out his
false teeth.

"Wfff rff nfff?" he mumbled, and quickly popped them back in. "Why on earth not?" he said. "Hats are brilliant things. You need one right away!" He grabbed his stick and disappeared into his bedroom.

"I've got just the one for you," he said,
taking a hat down from the top of his
wardrobe. "Had it for years! It's a Jones.
It's made for adventures!"

"And..." he paused to put the hat on Henry's head, "...it's also a great place to keep a secret."

It was a bit too big for

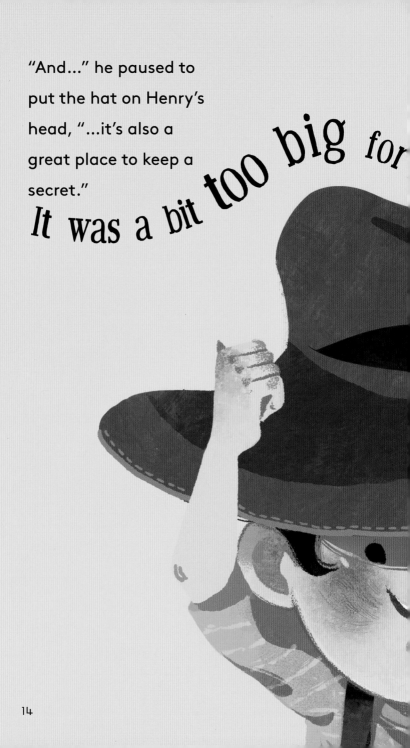

young Henry Pepper's head.

But Henry didn't
mind ... it wasn't
really for him
after all –

**it was for
the secret.**

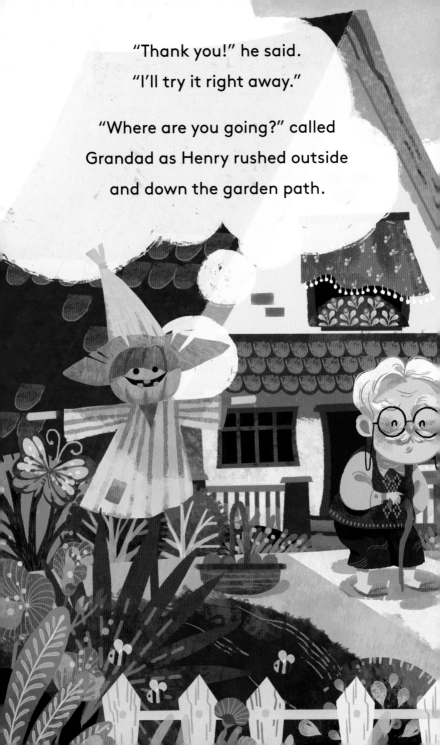

"Thank you!" he said.
"I'll try it right away."

"Where are you going?" called
Grandad as Henry rushed outside
and down the garden path.

"I'm going to put the secret under my hat ... like you said!"

Grandad chuckled.

"Come back home for lunch!"

CHAPTER 2

The hat was rather dusty and a bit worn round the edges.

Henry brushed off the dust, blew away the cobwebs, then turned it over and tap-tap-tapped its top.

"Much better,"
he said to
himself.

But just as he was about to put the hat back on, a strange sound rang out inside it – like a coin clattering around in a piggy bank – and then, with a creak, something

fell

out

and drifted slowly like a feather to the ground.

It was followed by another something...

... and another.

And a fourth,

and a fifth.

But they didn't all float to the ground
like the first ... they swirled up in
the air and then went off in different
directions ... too high to reach
and already on their way to
wherever they were going.

Henry quickly put the hat
back on his head.

And gulped.

By his feet was an old luggage label.

Henry picked it up and turned
it over.

Shh!
The Egg
Box Crown

What a strange thing!

he thought.

He read it again.

Could it be?

he wondered.

It had to be.

For the second time that morning Henry Pepper ran up the garden path of his Grandad's house and burst through the back door.

"Grandad," he puffed, "this fell out of your—"

Grandad Pepper was sat in his usual spot at the kitchen table and in his hand was another luggage label.

"This came in through the window," he said.

"I'm sorry, Grandad, I-I didn't mean to..."
Henry stuttered. "They all fell out of your
hat and floated away – all except this one.
It says 'number one'."

The old man smiled. **"They're my
secrets.** I kept them all under my hat,
you see. I had no idea they could escape!
I've got number four here," he added.
"And now I think about it, I remember this
one very well."

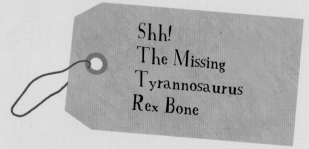

Shh!
The Missing
Tyrannosaurus
Rex Bone

"It's from years ago. Back when your
mum was still little herself. I was sitting
just here when I heard something in the
garden..." he began. "It was Fluffwell and
she was up to something."

"Fluffwell?"

asked Henry.

"Our dog. She had a nose for adventure!"
Grandad chuckled. "She was always
running away with my slipper, but this
time she'd gone for something a little bit
bigger...

"A dinosaur bone,
from the
museum!

I don't know how she got it – she was only a little dog – but there she was, trying to bury a Tyrannosaurus rex bone in the garden!"

"A T. rex!"

said Henry. "What did you do?"

"Well, everyone was looking for this bone, you see. It was on the radio. It was on the front page of the newspaper, too.

'DINOSAUR THIEF!' it said, but I didn't want that furry little thief Fluffwell to get into trouble...

So I waited until it was dark and then I took the bone back to the museum with a note to say 'sorry'.

"I didn't tell anyone about it. And from then on I let Fluffwell take my slipper whenever she wanted to!" Grandad chuckled again.

Just as the words were leaving his lips, the luggage label began to glow, and then *poof!* ... it turned into a T. rex and stomped away ... to dust.

"It's gone!" said Henry.

Grandad smiled. "It feels much
better now I've told someone about it.
And I'm glad that someone is you."

"I'm glad, too," said Henry.
"A T. rex!" he giggled.

"Now, what does your secret say?"
asked Grandad.

Henry read it again...

*Shh!
The Egg
Box Crown*

"Now this is a funny one!" said Grandad. "It was my first secret... Did I ever tell you about the day I met the Queen?"

"You met the Queen?"

gasped Henry.

"I was about the same age as you are now. The Queen was visiting our town. Everyone was talking about it. They put posters up in windows, planted flowers and hung up bunting from every street corner. The whole place was abuzz! My mum wore her smartest dress and my dad wore a bow tie. I wanted to wear something smart, too, but I didn't have a bow tie – or a smart dress! – so I made myself a crown out of an egg box and some buttons."

"Did the Queen
see it?" Henry asked.

"Oh! She did more than that!"
chortled Grandad. "On my way to
town, I passed the shiniest car I had ever
seen – a door opened and out stepped
the Queen. She was in a spot of bother,
you see – someone had forgotten to
pack her crown for the visit, and it just
so happened she had seen my crown
and, well, she asked if I would allow her
to wear it instead."

"The Queen wore
your egg-box
crown?" Henry
giggled.

"Yes! The whole day long!
And no one suspected a thing!"
said Grandad, reaching for the
biscuit tin.

"A few days later a parcel arrived,
addressed to me, and inside was a
note which read, 'Thank you. A hat for
a crown and a day saved'. It's the hat
that's on your head now," said Grandad.
"The Jones! It was a present from the
Queen."

As Grandad finished his story the
luggage label began to glow, just
like the one before it, and then, *poof!* ...
it folded up into a crown
and disappeared ... to dust.

Henry was speechless – and not just
because he had a mouthful of biscuit.

"It's your hat now," said Grandad, "but
you don't want a hat that's home to
my secrets, do you – even if they have
all escaped. We need to make room for
yours. Take another biscuit and let's go
and find the others, shall we?"

CHAPTER 3

Grandad wasn't the fastest walker but
Henry didn't mind – he had a lot of
questions to ask about Fluffwell and
the Queen. But before Grandad could
answer even one of them, they were
back at the place where the secrets had
fallen out of the hat.

"Did you see which way the others
went?" asked Grandad.

"One went left, one went right,
one went up the path to you and one
blew away down there," said Henry.

"Ah..." said Grandad.

"Do you think it's strange," said Henry,
"that the only secret which didn't float
away was the one about the hat itself?"

"...And the one that came home was about Fluffwell. They're all returning to the places they were made," said Grandad. "I think you're on to something, Henry."

"So, what's that way?"
Henry pointed down the path.

"Let's go and find out,"
said Grandad.

Grandad Pepper hadn't walked so far
in ages. He spent most days sat at the
kitchen table and the furthest he ever
went was to his greenhouse at the end
of the garden. His legs were stiff and his
knees ached but he was full of excitement
and energy for the adventure to come.

The path twisted and turned and opened
on to a village green, and beyond that, a
row of shops including a bakery.

"I think I know what the
next one is," said Grandad, licking
his lips.

The luggage label was exactly where Grandad said it would be – inside the baker's shop, tucked just behind the counter. Grandad kept the baker busy by ordering two Belgian buns, while Henry fetched the luggage label.

Then they found a bench outside to rest and eat, and read the next secret.

"Number two," said Grandad,

taking a bite of the bun.

Shh!
The Ice
and the
Polar Bear

"Have you ever been to the North Pole?" asked Grandad.

"No!" said Henry. "Have you?"

"Well, it just so happens I *have*..." said Grandad, wiping the corners of his mouth with his handkerchief. "You see, my dad was the baker here, once upon a time, and I helped him at weekends. Now, did you know the best iced cakes in the world are made with real ice from the North Pole? Not a lot of people know that." He nodded, taking another bite.

"I didn't know that," said Henry.

"The secret came one Saturday morning," Grandad continued, "when I opened the ice box delivery and discovered something else where the ice should be..."

"What was it?"

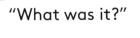"A polar bear!" said Grandad.
"A little cub."

"A real one?" asked Henry.

"Oh yes!" Grandad smiled. "But it couldn't stay here... And I still needed the ice for the cake I was making – so I took that polar bear home."

"WOW!" Henry almost dropped his bun!

"First we rode
my motorbike
all the way
to the sea...

Then I borrowed a rowing boat from a
fisherman and we

crossed the waves to the land
on the other side...

And there we found a sledge and some

dogs, and we

whooshed along the snowy hills...

...and out on to the ice, where the rest of that little polar bear's family were waiting."

"I bet they were pleased to see you!" said Henry.

"I'm not so sure! There was just enough time to grab some ice before I had to dash!" Grandad chuckled. "And when I got back I made the cake with my dad. It was a long day!"

"What a great adventure!" said Henry.

"One of my best ones!" Grandad
agreed as the luggage label began to glow,
and then *poof!* ... it turned into
a snowflake and floated
up, up and away ... to dust.

Grandad grabbed his stick once more.

"Three down, two to go," he said, striding out towards the old race track that lay beyond the trees beside the green.

"A long, long time ago, I dreamed of being a racing car driver," he said as the trees parted to reveal an overgrown track.

Henry laughed. "But you don't drive, Grandad..."

"I used to. I just don't any more. But I never raced again like then – the day my dream came true." He kicked up the dust. "I can still smell the tyres now."

As the dust settled by their feet, a luggage label landed on the ground in front of them.

"We beat it here!" said Grandad.

Shh!
The Fastest
Arrow

Henry picked it up. "It's number three!" he said. "What was the race?"

"It wasn't a race against other cars, it was a race against time," said Grandad. "Her name was the Arrow."

"She sounds fast!"

"Faster than anything ever before," Grandad said, walking the track.

"My friend Jude was the driver and all the world's press was there to watch her drive in record-breaking time. Dust swirled and flags waved. But just before she took her seat, Jude fell ill. She was devastated." Grandad sighed.

"There was a huge crowd waiting to see her – she couldn't disappoint them. So ... I took her driving helmet and goggles, and put them on, and I walked out on to the track as Jude."

"You drove the Arrow?" hooted Henry.

"For almost a year, I was the fastest person in the world! But nobody knew, except Jude and me. The next year Jude drove even faster and I was there to see her cross the line. I've never felt so proud to be beaten."

Henry ran off ahead
to cheer his grandad
across the finishing line.

"I wish I could have seen that,"

he said.

"Me too," said Grandad, taking the luggage label in his hand. He closed his eyes and smiled, and just as the others before it, the label began to glow, and then *poof!* ... it turned into the Arrow and sped off down the track ... to dust.

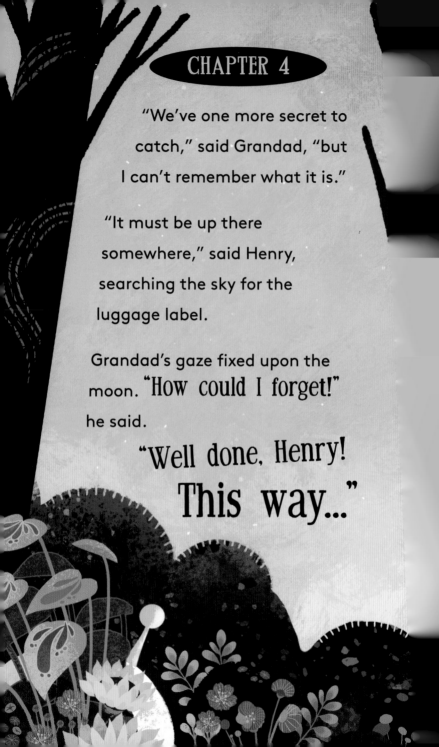

CHAPTER 4

"We've one more secret to catch," said Grandad, "but I can't remember what it is."

"It must be up there somewhere," said Henry, searching the sky for the luggage label.

Grandad's gaze fixed upon the moon. "How could I forget!" he said.

"Well done, Henry! This way..."

They left the track and crossed the
green in the opposite direction. All
the while, Henry listened as Grandad
told him everything he could
remember about the day he drove
the *Arrow*.

"This is the place," said Grandad as they entered through the sliding doors of the observatory.

"It all started here, with a rocket man."

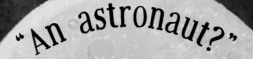

"An astronaut?"

Henry could hardly believe his own words. "You met an astronaut, too?" he said excitedly.

Grandad nodded and led the way down a corridor to a darkened room.

"This is the Moon Room,"

he said.

"Look!" said Henry,

"it's number five!"

On a model of the moon,
in the centre of the room,
was the

final luggage label.

Shh!
A Moon with
a View

As Grandad read the label, a big grin spread across his face. "This is my favourite one of all," he said.

"Your nanny loved everything about space. She read all the books and watched all the TV shows ... and she was sure she'd meet an alien one day!"

Henry's eyes widened as Grandad continued.

"Nanny used to come here every weekend. It's where we first met and it's where I had my best idea ever," he said, sitting down to rest.

"The astronaut had come to tell us all about the rocket he would fly into space and land on the moon. Nanny was completely starstruck! She told him how she dreamed of seeing the whole Earth, just like he would from up there in space, but she was afraid of heights, you see, so her chances weren't good!" said Grandad. "That's when I got the idea – I had a photo of Nanny in my pocket watch, so I waited till she was out of sight – and I asked that rocket man if he would take it to the moon."

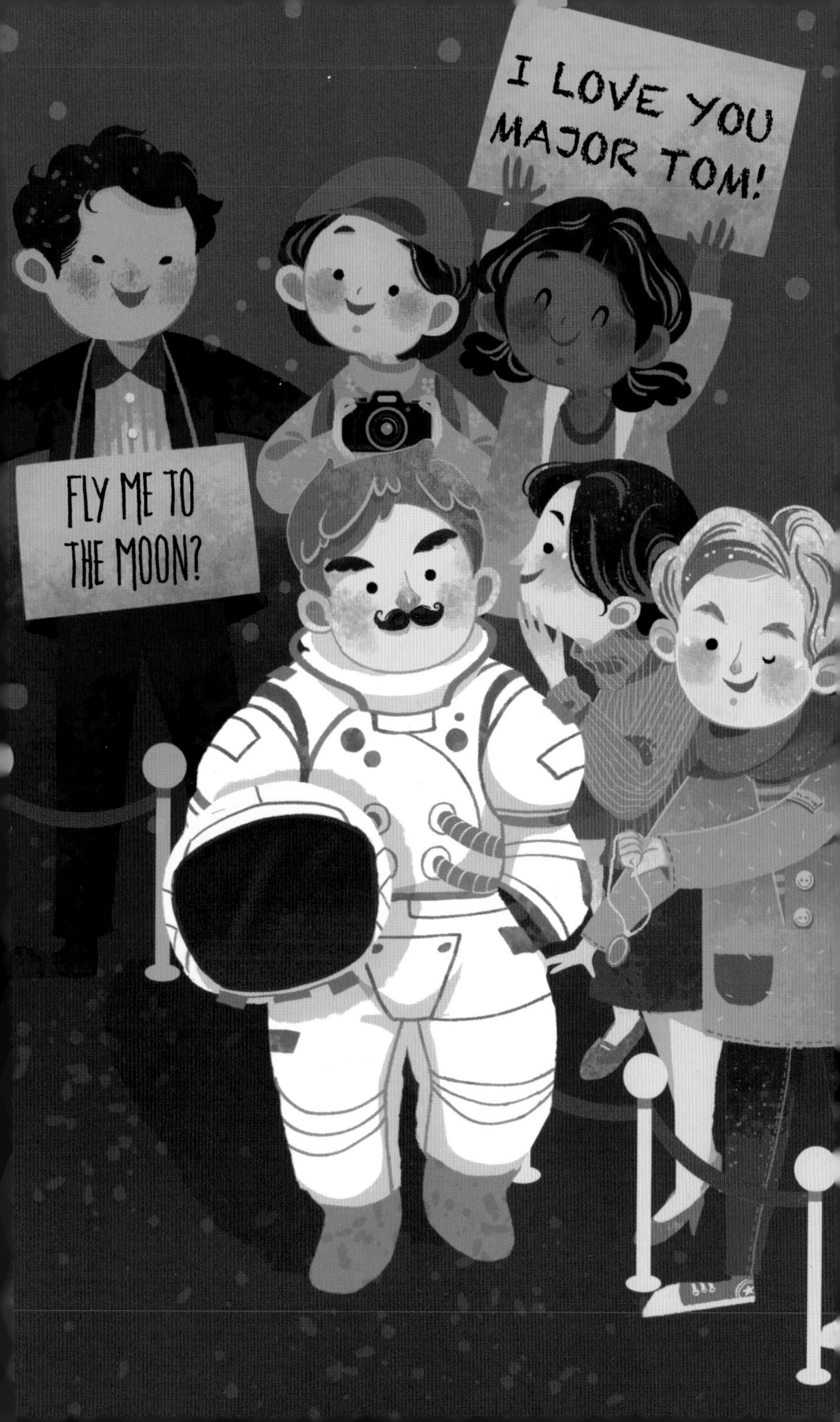
I LOVE YOU MAJOR TOM!
FLY ME TO THE MOON?

"No way!"

said Henry.

"Yes way!" Grandad replied.
"He snuck it in his space
suit and a few days later,
he landed on the moon and
he took it out, opened it up
and placed it down on the
surface.

And ever since then Nanny has been gazing at the whole Earth, just like she wanted to. Isn't it amazing?"

73

"I think that's the most amazing thing I have ever heard, EVER!" agreed Henry.

"Your nanny found out when the rocket man's postcard arrived. 'Oh, Mo!' she said. She was 'over the moon' you might say! We kept it a secret, though – we didn't want to get him in trouble. We used to gaze at the moon every night, knowing she was up there looking down at us. She's up there still," he smiled.

Henry beamed.

"It's our secret," said Grandad, giving the luggage label to Henry. "One for you to look after for me."

"I will," said Henry. "Always."

The luggage label in Henry's hand began
to glow so bright it lit up the Moon
Room, and then *poof!* ...
it turned into a rocket,
lifted off and was gone.

"The last one," said Grandad, patting
the hat on Henry's head. "It's ready
for your secret now," he said.

"I never imagined my own grandad could do all those amazing things," said Henry, helping the old man up.

"Adventure can find you in the most unusual ways," said Grandad, "and often when you're not even looking for it," he added as the sliding doors of the observatory opened and they started the walk home.

"There's more..." said Grandad as they crossed the green and headed back up the path. "More hats, I mean. I think there's even a couple of Nanny's up there on the wardrobe, too. Who knows what secrets she put under them? Aliens, I dare say!"

Henry.
Suddenly.
Stopped.

"Come on, I'll race you home – I was the fastest person in the world, you know!" quipped Grandad.

"Wait!" called Henry. "About the hat... I still haven't decided what to do."

"Oh!" said Grandad. "Well, don't let that secret eat you up. You can always tell me, you know?"

"But what if it eats you, too?"
said Henry.

Grandad winked. "I'm good with secrets. Now what is it?"

"It's... It's ... there!"
whispered Henry. "The thing. There it is!" he gulped, pointing through the trees beyond the brambles and bushes.

"Oh, that is a big one!"

said Grandad.

"That might just be the biggest secret I've ever seen."

He looked at Henry, wide-eyed.

"I think we're going to need a bigger hat!"

COLLECTIBLE STORIES
WITH COLOUR ILLUSTRATIONS

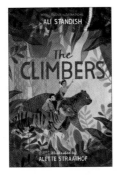